GRANDMA AND THE ANGRY OCTOPUS

Alison Grunwald

BLUE ROBIN PRESS

Illustration by Mike Phillips (Beehive Illustration).

With thanks to literary consultant Claire Wingfield for her
invaluable help.

Published by Blue Robin Press.

*Robins are loved for their beauty, speed and bravery. They are also
rather cunning and will dart in to steal a meal from a much larger bird
when it is not looking! They are mischievous, just like Grandma in these
stories, and they can't resist having a bit of fun.*

*We wondered what disguise a robin might use if it did not want to be
noticed, and the answer seemed obvious: it would mix up some blue
poster paint and jump right in. Who would recognise a blue robin?*

Imagine what naughty tricks it could get up to!

For Polly, Georgie, Thomas, Ben, Zoe, Grace, Jesse and Chloe, with all my love.

CONTENTS

1

GRANDMA'S BRIGHT IDEA

WHEN my Grandma looked out of her kitchen window, she was happy to see that the sun was shining brightly. There was Gertrude the cat, sunbathing contentedly on the patio, and the garden looked inviting.

Grandma opened the window and tapped her chin with a bony finger.

"Shall I do a spot of sunbathing? I could go out in the garden ... or perhaps it's a day for a swim?" she pondered.

Gertrude didn't much like water, so she hoped Grandma decided to stay at home. The sight of Grandma in her rainbow-coloured swimming costume was bad enough, without all that splashing around in the swimming pool. Turkish Van cats loved to swim, she knew, but she had

never been to Turkey to ask one how they did
it.

"That's settled then," announced my Grandma,
dashing into the garden. "We are heading to the
seaside."

"Oh cripes!" said Gertrude, which came out as
a loud "MIAOW."

But worse was to come. "I'll take my new
rainbow swimming costume," declared my
Grandma, decisively. "And my lovely orange
shower cap," she added.

"Oh no," miaowed Gertrude, covering her face
with her paws.

"Yes, I know you love coming with me,"
smiled Grandma, grabbing Gertrude before she
could make a run for it. "I'll just pop you in your
travel basket."

"Oh cripes," miaowed Gertrude again. This
was not going to end well, she thought.

And she was right.

2

GERTRUDE'S ESCAPE PLAN

It was a long train journey to the coast and Grandma whiled away the time by knitting.

Have I told you that my Grandma is a nit? Doh, I mean a knitter! She loves to knit, especially silly hats for babies in blue and pink. Today she had brought with her some fine yellow yarn as an experiment, and her knitting needles clacked away noisily.

What she didn't know was that the door to Gertrude's travel basket had silently opened and Gertrude was getting ready to pounce.

Cats love balls of wool and Grandma really didn't see it coming.

Up sprang Gertrude, a wild look in her eyes, her claws outstretched to grab on to the wool. She missed.

"AAAGH," screamed Grandma, as Gertrude's sharp claws sank into her lap.

A second later, things got even worse as the cat made a break for it, woollen ball in her mouth. Down the carriage she sped, the yellow wool unravelling behind her and Grandma's knitting needles jabbing the other passengers' ankles sharply.

Gertrude might have escaped the train completely but for the quick thinking of a boy who snatched her up and returned her to Grandma.

It took Grandma a long time to roll up the yellow wool and Gertrude spent the rest of the journey watching her progress with interest.

"That was great fun," she miaowed.

It was lucky for Gertrude that my Grandma didn't speak Cat ... but all that was about to change.

3

GRANDMA AND GERTRUDE
PLUNGE IN

On the beach my Grandma quickly undressed herself, her multi-coloured swimsuit dazzling all the nearby sunbathers, who reached for their sunglasses. With a final flourish, on went Grandma's bright orange shower-cap and Gertrude's pink lead.

"Just in time to put on our sun cream, Gertrude," exclaimed Grandma, slathering white lotion all over her face but forgetting to rub it in.

"She's going to look like a zebra," thought Gertrude, unkindly.

"Mustn't forget your nose, Gertrude," Grandma smiled with brilliant timing.

"Oh no! MIAOW," yelled Gertrude, hissing for added effect. It was too late; the sun cream had been blobbed onto her nose. It smelled awful and

Gertrude knew there was only one way to get rid of it.

Gertrude shot off towards the sea with my Grandma close behind, arms outstretched to grab her.

"Don't go in the water, Gertrude," she yelled. "You'll get all wet!"

"Don't care," screeched the cat, diving bravely through the waves to get rid of the annoying white lotion smeared over her delicate nose.

Grandma took a deep breath and, forgetting about her shower cap, dived in right behind Gertrude. And that's when things got very, very strange.

I don't know if you've ever swum in the sea? If you have, you probably know that you can't breathe underwater – and it's not a good idea to try.

Well, my Grandma opened her mouth to shout at Gertrude and found, to her amazement, that she was able to breathe. Not only that, Gertrude could breathe underwater too!

Even stranger still, my Grandma could now understand what Gertrude was saying! And their conversation went something like this ...

"Oh crumbs, I'm swimming and I'm not even Turkish!"

"Gertrude, just look around you at all the fish!"

"I'm off to catch one for my dinner."

"No, that's not a good idea, Gertrude."

"Why not?"

"Because of the octopus!" shrieked my Grandma.

4

"I'M A CATFISH"

"*What* octopus?" asked Gertrude, confused.

"The one right behind you, Gertrude. SWIM!!"

Even though she hadn't had a single lesson and she was definitely not from Turkey, Gertrude took off like a jet ski, paddling furiously away from a giant octopus that looked ready to pounce, with my Grandma in close pursuit.

Suddenly, a thunderous voice commanded: "STOP!"

"Oh cripes, this is bad," thought Gertrude. "We're going to get eaten for *his* supper."

But, if that was his plan, the angry octopus hadn't reckoned with my Grandma. Turning to face him, she took control of the situation.

"Good afternoon," she began, courteously.

"Very pleased to meet you. I'm Grandma and this is Gertrude."

The octopus was unimpressed. He stared at Gertrude fiercely.

"What sort of a fish are you?" he boomed.

"I'm a catfish," replied Gertrude, thinking quickly.

"No you're not!" countered the angry octopus.

"I've got cousins who are catfish – and they don't look like you."

"Well ... I'm a swimming cat, aren't I? So I must be a catfish."

Gertrude tried to sound convincing but found she was blowing bubbles each time she spoke, which didn't help.

"Catfish have very long whiskers," remarked the octopus, beginning to sound like a know-all.

"Well I've got long whiskers ... look." And Gertrude stuck her furry face in front of the octopus so he could have a closer look. It was a brave move.

"Well," conceded the sea giant. "You do look like a cat and you can swim. But unless you can both PROVE you are fish, I'm afraid I'll just have to eat you. It's in the rules. Sorry."

"Who makes the rules?" Grandma was indignant.

"I do. And I'm King around here," snapped the

octopus, waving his arms menacingly for emphasis. He wasn't used to fish that argued back.

5

NO JOKE

"Oh crikey. This is bad," said Gertrude, feeling trapped. She could never hope to swim as fast as a Turkish Van cat. Whatever was she going to do?

Grandma was not beaten yet. She adjusted her swimming costume, self-importantly.

"Ahem," she began, a plan forming in her mind.

"You are quite right, Sire – we aren't fish. But we do know some fishy jokes. Would that do?"

"For instance," she went on, pointing to her tummy. "Do you know how much this beautiful swimming costume cost me?"

"No idea," replied the octopus, looking bored. "Tell me."

"Fifteen squid," grinned my Grandma, a stream of silvery bubbles escaping from her mouth.

"Very funny, ha ha," commented the octopus in a sarcastic tone.

Grandma carried on, undaunted. "Why did the codfish blush?"

"Go on then, tell me," yawned the octopus.

"Because it saw the ocean's bottom," winked Grandma.

"That's bad, but I like it," remarked the octopus, despite himself.

Grandma was having fun now.

"What type of fish can make a violin sound better?" she asked.

"That's a hard one," grumbled the octopus. "Tell me."

"A tuna," laughed Grandma, in her element now.

The octopus rolled his eyes and it was difficult to know know what that meant.

"Any more?" he asked.

"What do you get from an angry shark?"

"I dunno," the octopus replied. "What *do* you get from an angry shark?"

"As far away as possible," quipped my Grandma.

"What do sea monsters eat?" she continued, not wanting to lose her advantage.

"Go on, tell me," prompted the octopus.

"Fish and ships!"

"Oh that's bad too," the octopus remarked, his voice sounding a *bit* less angry.

6

TIME FOR SUPPER

Grandma didn't stop there – she had a feeling things were going her way.

"Where does a fish keep his money?" she asked, sweetly.

"I don't know. Where *does* a fish keep his money?" responded the octopus.

"In the river bank," Grandma chortled.

"What do you call a fish that has two knees?" she went on.

The octopus looked stuck. "Go on then," he replied. "What's the answer?"

"A tunee fish," grinned Grandma, doing her best to slap her knees.

"Just one more joke before it's time for supper," remarked the octopus, nastily.

Grandma decided it was now or never, and she would have to risk it ...

"How many tickles does it take to make an octopus laugh?"

"I don't know," said the octopus, beginning to glare again. "You'll have to tell me."

"Tentacles," said my Grandma, getting ready to make a break for it. Things were looking pretty bleak. "Can I sing you a song?" she added sweetly.

"This is not going to end well," thought Gertrude, sticking her paws into her ears. (If you have ever heard my Grandma sing, you'll understand why.)

Taking a deep breath, my Grandma launched into her song ...

"Baa baa black ship ..."

The octopus was not amused. He raised one of his arms like a stop sign.

"That's just babyish," he sneered.

He had begun to tie a napkin around his neck and Gertrude didn't like it.

Grandma tried a final tune. "How about: 'The whales on the bus go round and round!'" she sang, sounding like two violins crashing into one another.

GET OUT OF MY SEA!

"ENOUGH," thundered the octopus, sticking all of his eight arms into his ears at once so that he looked like a football gone wrong.

"That's it. Get out of my sea, NOW, before I

change my mind. And take that strange looking catfish with you!"

Scrambling out of the sea as fast as they could, Grandma and Gertrude lay on the wet sand, breathing fast and feeling thankful to have survived.

Feeling for her frizzy red hair, Grandma realised for the first time that she wasn't wearing her orange shower cap any longer.

"I wonder where my shower cap ended up," she said to herself.

"Miaow," replied Gertrude, knowingly.

"You'll have to ask the octopus that one," she smiled to herself.

NOW IT'S TIME TO PUT ON YOUR THINKING CAPS!

1. In *Grandma and the Angry Octopus*, what sort of person do you think Grandma is? How would you describe her?

2. At the beginning of the story, Gertrude thinks about a type of cat that loves to swim. Do you remember which country this cat comes from?

3. Why did the sunbathers on the beach reach for their sunglasses when they saw Grandma?

4. Why did Gertrude dash into the sea in a hurry?

5. What sort of mood was the octopus in when he noticed Grandma and Gertrude? Was he happy, bossy, annoyed, proud? Can you think of more ways to describe him?

6. How did Gertrude convince the octopus that she was a catfish?

7. Why do you think the octopus tied a napkin round his neck?

8. According to Grandma, where does a fish keep his money?

9. What made the octopus look like a football gone wrong?

10. What did Grandma lose at the end of the story? Where did it go?

ABOUT THE AUTHOR

Alison Grunwald has always loved writing comic stories and poems for children. She enjoyed working in primary schools teaching early reading to children arriving from other countries. One of the ways she did this was by inventing and singing a rap which made them laugh and helped them learn vowel sounds!

Alison has been a radio and newspaper reporter and a doula. This is someone who looks after mums when they are expecting a baby and helps them learn how to feed and look after it. Sometimes twins arrive and Alison knows what to do because she has twins herself!

These days Alison has lots of grandchildren who help her with suggestions for her funny stories. Would you like to write a story for her to read? Here are a few ideas to get you going!

Decide who and what the tale is about; find a comfortable place to write or type; build your story with plenty of interest; use great descriptions and remember to end your tale as well as it started.

You can get in touch with Alison via email at: a.grunwald@btinternet.com to send your stories, jokes or just to say hello. (Please get permission from a grown-up before sending your email.)

If you enjoyed this book, please look out for more of Grandma and Gertrude's adventures, and please help to spread the word by telling your friends, teachers, pets and grandmas. You might even like to write a book review and send it to Alison. She would love to hear from you – but for now, it's until the next time from Alison, Grandma and Gertrude!